# PEANUTS®
## LUCY
## Knows Best

by Charles M. Schulz

adapted by Kama Einhorn

illustrated by Robert Pope

Ready-to-Read

Simon Spotlight
New York   London   Toronto   Sydney   New Delhi

SIMON SPOTLIGHT
An imprint of Simon & Schuster Children's Publishing Division
1230 Avenue of the Americas, New York, New York 10020
This Simon Spotlight edition August 2016
© 2016 Peanuts Worldwide LLC
SIMON SPOTLIGHT, READY-TO-READ, and colophon are registered trademarks of Simon & Schuster, Inc.
For information about special discounts for bulk purchases, please contact Simon & Schuster Special Sales at
1-866-506-1949 or business@simonandschuster.com.
Manufactured in the United States of America 0716 LAK
2 4 6 8 10 9 7 5 3 1
ISBN 978-1-4814-6771-1 (hc)
ISBN 978-1-4814-6770-4 (pbk)
ISBN 978-1-4814-6772-8 (eBook)

Lucy has a booth where she helps friends with their problems. Lucy gives lots of advice, and it only costs five cents!

Charlie Brown is Lucy's biggest customer.
"Why are you so good at helping people?" he asks.

Lucy lifts her chin proudly.
"I know everything!" she says.
"That's a good reason,"
says Charlie Brown.
"I'm glad you agree," says Lucy.
"How can I help you today?"

THE DOCTOR

IS IN

Charlie Brown wants to feel
confident, like Lucy.
"Try whistling," Lucy says.
"You'll feel better about
yourself and everyone around you."

Charlie Brown walks home,
whistling. He feels better!
Then he passes Woodstock,
whistling a fancier tune.
Charlie Brown stops whistling.
He doesn't feel as good
about himself anymore.

Charlie Brown goes back to Lucy.
"I think I need another suggestion,"
he says.
"You're hopeless," she says. "Next!"

"Will you help my dog, Snoopy?
He can't sleep because he's afraid of
the dark," says Charlie Brown.
"I'll help anyone with five cents!"
Lucy says.

Snoopy comes to see Lucy.
"The dark can't hurt you,"
says Lucy.
Snoopy falls asleep at the booth!
"Stay awake when I'm talking
to you!" screams Lucy.

PSYCHIATRIC
HELP 5¢

THE DOCTOR
IS IN

"Give me your paw,"
Lucy says. "Say to yourself:
I am loved. I am needed.
I am important."
Snoopy feels better holding Lucy's
hand. He smiles!
Lucy sends him home.

At home Snoopy finds Woodstock.
Woodstock looks sad.
Snoopy knows what to do!

Snoopy brings Woodstock to see Lucy.
"Good grief! Why are you so mopey?" she says. "You're a bird! You can fly! Remember . . . there's a great big sky out there!"

THE DOCTOR

Lucy is right! Woodstock flaps
his little wings and takes off.
"Rats!" Lucy says. "I helped
him so fast, he flew
away without paying!"

Next Lucy's friend Schroeder has a problem.
"I want to go to summer music camp, but I don't know how to get there," he says.

THE DOCTOR IS IN

Lucy thinks Schroeder is cute.
She helps him really quickly.
"I've booked you on flight
fifty-four, first class!" she says,
handing him a ticket.

"Wow," Schroeder says. "You are so helpful."
"Yes, I'll even kiss you good-bye!" Lucy says.

Lucy leans in for a kiss,
but Schroeder ignores her.
"I have to look for a magazine
to read on the plane," he says.

Lucy is disappointed.
When Schroeder comes back
from camp, she tries again
to get his attention.

"I read that our arms weren't made for throwing baseballs," Lucy says. "Really?" Schroeder asks. "What are arms made for?"

"Hugging!" Lucy grins.
Schroeder rolls his eyes
and says, "BLEAH!"

Ugh! Lucy is angry with Schroeder. She stomps home to sulk. She crawls into her beanbag chair and sinks all the way down. She needs advice. Who can she ask?

Herself!
Lucy goes to her own booth.
"I need some help," she says out
loud.

Then Lucy moves behind the booth. "Good. That's why I'm here," she answers.

THE DOCTOR IS IN

Lucy moves to the other
side of the booth. "There's this
boy I like, but he never notices me,"
she says.
"It makes me sad."

Lucy moves behind the booth
again. "What's the problem?" she
asks. "You're smart and beautiful.
You shouldn't chase after anyone!"

"Do you really think so?"
Lucy asks.
"Of course!" she says from behind
the booth. "I wouldn't lie to you!"
That's just what Lucy needs to hear!

She walks straight to Schroeder's house.
On the way she thinks about how smart she is. She fixes everyone's problems. Crummy old Schroeder only cares about his music.

"I got advice from the smartest person I know. Want to know what she said?" Lucy asks. Schroeder ignores her. Lucy sticks out her tongue. "She said . . . BLEAH!"

Lucy goes back to her
booth feeling great.
After all, Lucy knows best!